KINGS & QUEENS

BOOK IV

1714 ~ PRESENT DAY

THE MILLENNIUM SERIES

by

John Guy

GEORGE I

BORN 1660 • ACCEDED 1714 • DIED 1727

George I was the first Hanoverian monarch of Britain, marking a period of great change in the constitution. In 1701 the Act of Settlement had been passed which ensured that a Catholic monarch could never again sit on the British throne. When Anne died in 1714 without leaving an heir, she was the last Stuart monarch and succession passed to George of Hanover, great-grandson of James I and Anne's distant cousin, her closest relative. George had little interest in Britain and could speak no English, so it became necessary for many of his governmental duties to be transferred to Parliament and his ministers.

SIR ROBERT WALPOLE (1676-1745)

A member of the Whig (Liberal) party, Sir Robert Walpole dominated British political life, particularly during the period 1721-42. As George became more and more reliant on his politicians to govern the country, Walpole took the opportunity of increasing the power and influence of the House of Commons. In 1721 he became the First Lord of the Treasury, the most powerful position in Parliament, and became, in effect, the first Prime Minister.

JACOBITE REBELLION (1715)

George's accession to the British throne was not a popular choice, especially in Scotland, where a rebellion broke out to place a Stuart back on the throne. The rebellion was led by James Edward Stuart, son of the deposed James II, known as the 'Old Pretender'. The rising did not progress beyond Scotland and was soon put down.

SOUTH SEA BUBBLE

In 1711 a speculative company was set up to trade with South America, under a treaty with Spain. The Government invested heavily and encouraged many others to do likewise. Many thousands, in the hope of becoming rich, invested their savings in the company, which became grossly over-subscribed. When the 'bubble burst' in 1720, many faced financial ruin.

1714	Townsend and Robert	Stuart, the 'Old Pretender'	1717	1718
George I succeeds his cousin Anne to the throne.	Walpole as leaders.	on the throne.	Sir Robert Walpole resigns from	Quadruple Alliance between Britain,
1714	1715	1716	government following	France, Austria
New Whig government elected with Charles	Jacobite rebellion in Scotland fails in its attempt to put James	The Septennial Act calls for General Elections every seven years.	Townsend's dismissal from the government.	and Netherlands against Spain.

 ARCHITECTURE 📖 ARTS & LITERATURE ⚑ EXPLORATION 💥 FAMOUS BATTLES

📖 SAMUEL JOHNSON (1709-84)

A writer, critic and lexicographer (someone who studies words), Samuel Johnson is famous for compiling the first proper 'Dictionary of the English Language'. First published in 1755, it took him 9 years to compile and contained over 40,000 entries.

📜 SEPTENNIAL ACT

In 1716 The Septennial Act was passed in Parliament which decreed that General Elections should be held every seven years. This level of freedom to vote for one's government was unheard of in George's native Germany, and most of Europe, at the time.

📖 DANIEL DEFOE (1660-1731)

Daniel Defoe started his writing career as a pamphleteer (what we today would term a journalist) and was imprisoned for his outspoken views. It was during a spell in prison that he wrote 'Robinson Crusoe' (below), which was published in 1719 and is generally regarded by most as the first truly great English novel.

WILLIAM HOGARTH (1697-1764)

William Hogarth became the most important English artist of his time, turning away from foreign influences and establishing a style of his own. He painted a series of pictures which told a sequence of contemporary moral tales, establishing him as both an artist and a satirist. He went on to produce a series of sharply witty and satirical engravings which are important for the subject matter they portray, like the hypocrisy of religion, the horror of asylums (above) and the appalling social conditions of the day.

SOPHIA DOROTHEA

George married Sophia Dorothea, the beautiful but arrogant daughter of his countryman, the Duke of Celle, in 1682, before he became King of England. It was a loveless marriage and after she bore him two children they went their separate ways. George had several illicit liaisons, while Sophia had an affair with Count Philip von Konigsmarck, of Sweden. Despite having mistresses of his own, George was infuriated. He had the Count killed and banished his wife from court.

1719
'Robinson Crusoe' published by Daniel Defoe; generally regarded as first 'great' novel.
1720
South Sea Bubble, a

speculative company, bursts, causing widespread financial ruin.
1721
Sir Robert Walpole reinstated and becomes

first Prime Minister as First Lord of the Treasury.
1722
Duke of Marlborough dies.
1725
Treaty of Hanover,

forms an alliance between Britain, France, Prussia and other northern European countries.
1726
Edinburgh opens

first circulating library.
1727
Sir Isaac Newton dies.
1727
George I dies.

📜 GOVERNMENT   ⚗ HEALTH & MEDICINE   ⚖ JUSTICE   ✝ RELIGION   📗 SCIENCE

GEORGE II

BORN 1683 • ACCEDED 1727 • DIED 1760

*U*nder the expert guidance of Robert Walpole the first third of George's reign was one of peace and great prosperity. The Prime Minister skilfully steered Britain away from all wars in Europe, but after he retired from politics, the remainder of George's reign was spent in one conflict or another, including war with Spain and two separate conflicts with France. During his reign also, the British Empire acquired considerable new domains.

JAMES WOLFE

James Wolfe, although of a frail constitution, proved a courageous and extremely capable commander. He joined the army as a boy and by the age of 16 had already become an officer. He quickly rose through the ranks to become a captain at 17, lieutenant-colonel at 23 and major general soon after. He was actively involved in the 'Seven Years' War' with France and led the attack on Quebec in 1759, which secured Canada as part of the British Empire, though he was killed in the process.

WILLIAM PITT THE ELDER (1708-78)

Of humble birth, William Pitt was known as the 'Great Commoner'. He was a politician of rare genius, though he suffered from ill-health, including bouts of mental illness, which may have impaired his judgement on occasion. He became Prime Minister of a coalition government in 1757 and again, as a Whig, between 1766-67. As Secretary of State he led Britain to victory against France in the 'Seven Years' War', establishing Britain as the most powerful world power.

CAROLINE OF BRANDENBURG-ANSBACH

George married Caroline in 1705 and together they had 10 children. She remained faithful to him, even though he had numerous affairs. He never remarried after her death in 1737. She was plump, but not unattractive, and possessed great charm and intelligence, striking up a life-long, though strictly professional, friendship with Robert Walpole.

1727 George II succeeds his father to the throne.	**1736** Witchcraft abolished as a crime.	**1739** War of Captain Jenkins' Ear breaks out with Spain.	**1742** Sir Robert Walpole resigns as Prime Minster.	Dettingen, Bavaria, one of the last occasions when ruling monarch led troops in war.
1732 Royal Charter issued to found Georgia in America.	**1738** Wesley brothers found the Methodist movement.	**1740** War of Austrian Succession breaks out.	**1743** George leads his army into battle at	**1745** Sir Robert Walpole dies.

 ARCHITECTURE    ARTS & LITERATURE   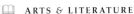 EXPLORATION   FAMOUS BATTLES

JACOBITE REBELLION (1745)

The second Jacobite rebellion, although ending in failure, was a much more serious attempt to place the Catholic Stuarts back on the throne. The word Jacobite comes from the Latin word for James, 'Jacobus', and is the name adopted by the supporters of James II and his heirs. This second rising was led by Charles Edward Stuart (the 'Young Pretender') known as 'Bonnie Prince Charlie'. He achieved early success against the English at the Battle of Prestonpans in July 1745 but by the following April he was defeated. He escaped to exile in France (aided by Flora Macdonald) and died penniless in 1788.

WITCHCRAFT

In country areas, many of the old ways, such as herbal remedies, were still practised and many villages supported a local 'wise-woman'. Such things were little understood by the church and the authorities, who saw it as witchcraft. Until 1712 the practising of witchcraft was still punishable by death and it remained a crime right up until 1736.

WAR OF CAPTAIN JENKINS'S EAR

In 1739 Britain declared war with its old enemy Spain. The incident which is said to have sparked off the conflict took place during a skirmish in the South Seas. Spain had long been subjected to piratical raids by the English and during one such raid an English captain named Jenkins had his ear cut off. Whether or not the story is true is debatable, but open hostilities did break out between the two countries.

BRITISH MUSEUM

As an outward show of Britain's growing Empire and world power, a new, national museum was founded in London in 1753, known as the British Museum. It opened six years later and was partly paid for out of proceeds from a lottery. In addition to displaying artefacts gathered from the colonies, the museum quickly became regarded as one of the finest such educational institutions in the world.

📖 HANDEL (1685-1759)

George Frederick Handel, musician and composer, came to live in England in 1712 and soon became a favourite at court. His great love was for choral works, several based on Biblical stories, such as 'The Messiah', first performed in 1742, and 'Music for Royal Fireworks', performed in 1748 to celebrate the end of the war of the Austrian Succession.

✝ JOHN WESLEY (1703-91)

John Wesley, together with his brother Charles, founded a new, non-conformist Protestant church known as the Methodists, so called because of their strict religious observance. The order was formed by Charles in 1738, but it was when John Wesley joined the movement soon afterwards that it really caught the popular imagination. Wesley was a fine orator and frequently gave open-air sermons which attracted huge audiences of 20,000 or more.

💣 BATTLE OF CULLODEN

The hopes and dreams of the Jacobite rebels came to an end at the Battle of Culloden in April 1746. The English, under the Duke of Cumberland, inflicted a massive defeat on the Scots, thus ending the Stuart claim to the throne once and for all. For many years after, even the wearing of kilts and the playing of bagpipes was punishable by death.

🏴 CLIVE OF INDIA (1725-74)

At the same time as Wolfe was winning victories against the French in North America, Robert Clive was doing likewise in India. In 1757 he won the Battle of Plessey thus adding India to the Empire, and was appointed governor of Bengal. However, he was hated by the Indians and was censured for misgovernment; he later committed suicide in London.

1745 Second Jacobite rebellion meets with Scottish victory at Prestonpans. **1746** Jacobites beaten at	*Battle of Culloden.* **1751** *George's eldest son, Frederick, dies. His son, George becomes heir.*	**1753** *British Museum founded in London.* **1756/63** *Seven Years' War with France.*	**1757** *Robert Clive acquires Indian province of Bengal for Britain.* **1757** *William Pitt, the Elder, becomes Prime Minister.*	**1759** *Wolfe captures Quebec from French; secures Canada as English colony.* **1760** *George II dies.*

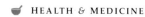

📜 GOVERNMENT   ⚕ HEALTH & MEDICINE   ⚖ JUSTICE   ✝ RELIGION   📘 SCIENCE

📖 JANE AUSTEN

Jane Austen (1775-1817) was a clergyman's daughter from Hampshire who liked to write stories as a young girl to amuse herself. Several of these, including 'Pride and Prejudice', were later reworked as socially witty novels. She wrote from personal experience only so her work gives us valuable insights into the snobbery and morality of Georgian society.

📜 ACT OF UNION WITH IRELAND

During the 17th and 18th centuries many Protestants had been encouraged to settle in Ireland to help keep the country loyal to England. In 1798 a rebellion to unite Catholics and Protestants against England failed. In response, the Act of Union was passed in 1800 making Ireland part of the U.K.

🏴 AUSTRALIA DISCOVERED

Although Dutch sailors had discovered Australia some time before, it was the voyages of Captain Cook between 1768-79 that opened up the country for colonisation. Many new plants and animals were discovered, including the kangaroo.

THE FRENCH REVOLUTION

The growing tide of social unrest in Europe resulted, in 1798, in open revolution in France, leading to the eventual overthrow of the monarchy and the execution of Louis XVI.

A DEVOTED QUEEN

On 8th September 1761 George married Charlotte of Mecklenburg-Strelitz. Tradition has it that it was an arranged marriage and they met for the first time only on the afternoon of the wedding. The early years of their marriage were very happy and they had 15 children. Charlotte was intelligent and vivacious in her youth, but became quite obese in later life. She grew to love George and remained devoted to him throughout his earlier bouts of illness, but gradually grew away from him in later life. Sadly, the king did not recognise her when she died in 1818 aged 75.

KEW PALACE

In 1730 Kew House and gardens were acquired by George III. His mother, Princess Augusta, began a nine acre botanical garden and study centre there in 1759.

A PRIME MINISTER ASSASSINATED

On 12th May 1812 Spencer Perceval, the Prime Minister, was assassinated in the lobby of the House of Commons by an insane bankrupt, Francis Bellingham.

1760	**1763**	colonies and leads	around the world.	**1783**
George III succeeds his	Seven Years War ends	eventually to War of	**1773**	America recognised
grandfather as king.	with 'Peace of Paris'.	American Independence.	Boston Tea Party.	by Britain as a nation
1760	**1765**	**1769/70**	**1775/83**	in own right.
Start of the Industrial	Stamp Act raises	James Cook's first epic	American War of	**1783**
Revolution in Britain.	taxes in American	voyage of discovery	Independence.	William Pitt, the Younger,

🏛 ARCHITECTURE   📖 ARTS & LITERATURE   🏴 EXPLORATION   🔥 FAMOUS BATTLES

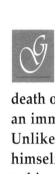

GEORGE III

BORN 1738 • ACCEDED 1760 • DIED 1820

George III was the first of the Hanoverian monarchs to be born in England. He succeeded to the throne in 1760 on the death of his grandfather, George II, and took an immediate interest in affairs of state. Unlike his two predecessors, he regarded himself as English and the people warmed to his simple, direct manner. He was plagued by ill health in later years and in 1811 his son was created Prince Regent. His long reign spanned almost the entire period now termed the 'Industrial Revolution' and saw many changes, but he is perhaps best remembered for the loss of the American colonies in 1783.

FARMER GEORGE

George always regarded himself as an ordinary man. He was very hard-working and took a strong interest in government. From an early age he also showed a keen interest in farming and liked to chat to workers on the royal farms, earning him the nickname 'Farmer George'.

THE NAPOLEONIC WARS

Within a few years of the French Revolution, France began to assert itself as a major power in Europe, under the leadership of Napoleon Bonaparte. War broke out between Britain and France in 1793 and resumed again in 1803, after a short truce. Napoleon was finally defeated at the Battle of Waterloo in 1815.

MENTAL ILLNESS

From 1788 George suffered periods of mental instability and was kept locked away. Modern research, however, would suggest that he was not mad but suffering from porphyria.

becomes Prime Minister.
1789
Outbreak of French Revolution.
1793
War breaks out between Britain and France again.

1800
Act of Union passed between Britain and Ireland.
1803/15
Napoleonic Wars between England and France,

1805
Nelson defeats French at Battle of Trafalgar.
1811
George III's son become Regent during prolonged

spell of illness.
1812
Spencer Perceval, Prime Minister, assassinated.
1815
Napoleon defeated

at Battle of Waterloo.
1815
Corn Laws passed.
1820
George III dies.

📗 GOVERNMENT   ⚗ HEALTH & MEDICINE   ⚖ JUSTICE   ✝ RELIGION   📘 SCIENCE

LOSS OF THE AMERICAN COLONIES
(1775-1783)

*T*he American War of Independence was the first colonial revolt in the British Empire. The government at home completely misread the situation, scarcely believing that such a revolt was possible. The revolt could perhaps have been avoided if they had listened to the grievances of the colonists, especially with regard to taxes, and when the French supported them against the English, the conclusion was inevitable. Although the war did not finally end until 1783, after eight years of bitter struggle, the outcome was effectively decided after the British surrender of Yorktown two years previously in 1781.

GEORGE WASHINGTON
(1732-99)

George Washington was born in Virginia and traced his ancestry back to a Northamptonshire farming family. He fought for the English in the French and Indian wars of 1754-63. In 1775 he was made commander-in-chief of Continental forces and led the revolution against England. He became the first President of the newly founded United States of America and served two terms between 1787-97. He refused a third term and retired to his home at Mount Vernon, Virginia.

GEORGE III

George III was the last British monarch to preside over the American colonies. His Prime Minister, Lord North, proved incapable of handling the situation properly and is held to be largely responsible for the loss of the colonies by misreading the seriousness of the revolt.

ALLIANCE WITH FRANCE

In 1777, following the British defeat at Saratoga, the French recognised the American states as an independent nation and sent military aid. The British and French had long been engaged in war across the globe, fiercely contesting colonial rule and the American war presented a golden opportunity for France to deliver a crushing blow to her old adversary.

🏛 ARCHITECTURE   📖 ARTS & LITERATURE   🏴 EXPLORATION   💥 FAMOUS BATTLES

BOSTON TEA PARTY

The action that prompted the start of the War of Independence began in 1765 with the Stamp Act, which increased taxes dramatically in the American colonies. It was followed five years later by the Boston Massacre, when British troops opened fire on a group of rebelling, but unarmed civilians, killing five. The situation rapidly worsened and in December 1773 a group of colonists disguised themselves as Indians and emptied the contents of over 300 tea chests into Boston harbour in protest at the high taxes imposed by the British government. Open conflict began in 1775.

SARATOGA

The early engagements of the war went well for the British and for a while it looked as though the revolt would be easily put down. The tide of the war turned in 1777, however, when General Howe suffered a humiliating defeat at the hands of the colonists, under Washington, at the Battle of Saratoga.

YORKTOWN

The Battle of Yorktown, Virginia, fought on 19th October 1781, marked the real end of the war. The British, led by General Cornwallis, became cut off by a combined American and French force greatly superior in numbers. The humiliated Cornwallis was forced to surrender. It was the last major battle of the war and although the British fought on in a number of minor skirmishes, the position was hopeless and the outcome of the war had already been decided. The British are shown (left) surrendering to General Washington in 1781. Britain recognised the independence of the American colonies.

DECLARATION OF INDEPENDENCE

In protest at the British government's implementation of high taxes from far-off London, the colonists revolted claiming that there should be 'no taxation without representation'. The Declaration of Independence was issued on 4th July 1776 following a delegation, headed by Thomas Jefferson and Benjamin Franklin, at the Continental Congress.

GOVERNMENT   HEALTH & MEDICINE   JUSTICE   RELIGION   SCIENCE

🗡 CATO STREET CONSPIRACY

In 1820, in the wake of the French Revolution, a plot was hatched by a group of conspirators, led by Arthur Thistlewood, to assassinate the entire British cabinet. Thistlewood was to be proclaimed president of a new-style of government, but the plotters were betrayed and they were arrested at their headquarters in Cato Street, London.

📖 NATIONAL GALLERY

George was a great patron of the arts, commissioning many paintings and works of architecture. He established the National Gallery in London in 1824 in which to house a national collection of art, accessible to all.

FIRST PUBLIC RAILWAY

Thomas Newcomen developed the first practical steam engine about 1712 and the first successful steam-powered locomotives were built in 1808 by Richard Trevithick, a Cornish mining engineer. The first railway to use steam from the start was the Stockton-Darlington Railway, which opened in 1825 followed, in 1833, by the world's first public railway.

MRS. FITZHERBERT

The Act of Settlement, passed in 1701, forbade George (heir to the throne) to marry a Catholic, but he married his Catholic mistress, Maria Fitzherbert, in secret in 1785. The marriage was never officially recognised and the Reverend Robert Burt, who performed the ceremony in London, was later transferred to the remote marshland parish of St.Mary Hoo, near Rochester in Kent, to live out his life in obscurity.

TURNPIKE ROADS

In the Georgian period Britain's roads had fallen into a shocking state of repair. A series of laws was passed which allowed for Turnpike Trusts to be formed. Their purpose was to build new roads with stone and tarmacadam surfaces, paid for by charging a toll to all those who used them. They were hated by the poor and the drovers, who could not afford the tolls, but by 1830 there were over 20,500 miles (33,000 kilometres) of turnpike roads in Britain.

ROBERT PEEL

The first organised civilian police force was introduced in London in 1829 by Sir Robert Peel, later Prime Minister. There had been various attempts at patrolling the streets against crime since the Middle Ages, but the 'Peelers', as they came to be known, were the first force to be properly recruited and paid for from public funds. Many of those recruited were ex-servicemen, home from the wars, and the force was run along military lines.

1820	Conspiracy threatens	1821	Niepce on a metal plate.	1823
George IV accedes to	to overthrow	Queen Caroline excluded	**1822**	Francis Ronalds invents
the throne after many	government.	from George's coronation.	William Church invents	first electric telegraph.
years as Regent.	**1820**	**1822**	a typesetting machine	**1823**
1820	Trial of Queen Caroline	First photograph taken	which streamlines the	Construction begins on
Cato Street	for adultery.	by Joseph Nicephore	publishing of books.	the British Museum

🏛 ARCHITECTURE　📖 ARTS & LITERATURE　🏴 EXPLORATION　💣 FAMOUS BATTLES

GEORGE IV

BORN 1762 • ACCEDED 1820 • DIED 1830

Having spent the better part of his life in his father's shadow, George IV's reign was a comparatively short one. Always prone to excesses, particularly during his Regency, he changed from a handsome, popular prince into a debauched and obese caricature of his former self. As part of a deal to get Parliament to pay off his mounting debts, George had to marry his cousin, Caroline of Brunswick, in 1795. It was a loveless match and George refused to allow her to be present at his Coronation.

THE REGENCY

George's father, George III, suffered frequent bouts of what was then thought to be madness, but is now generally recognised as porphyria. During these periods, the ageing king was considered unfit to govern. In 1811 his son became Regent, as Prince George, taking over many of the constitutional roles of his father.

BRIGHTON PAVILION

Whilst still Prince Regent, George commissioned John Nash to redesign his seaside home at Brighton (where he stayed when taking his regular sea-water health cures) and convert it into a palace. Nash used his skill and ingenuity to unify the Prince's fascination with oriental and Indian art into the extravaganza of Brighton Pavilion, which still survives intact.

1824	Stockton and Darlington.	sets up the world's	in London.	**1830**
National Gallery founded	**1828**	first organised	**1829**	George Stephenson's
in London.	The Duke of Wellington	police force.	Catholic Relief	'Rocket' wins 'Rainhill
1825	becomes Prime Minister.	**1829**	Act passed, allowing	Trials' in Liverpool.
World's first public railway	**1829**	First horse-drawn	Catholics to	**1830**
system is opened between	Sir Robert Peel	buses appear	become M.P.s.	George IV dies.

🏛 GOVERNMENT   ⚕ HEALTH & MEDICINE   ⚖ JUSTICE   ✝ RELIGION   🔬 SCIENCE

WILLIAM IV

BORN 1765 • ACCEDED 1830 • DIED 1837

As the third son of George III, William could never have expected to become king and only did so, at the age of 64, on the death of his brother, George. His short reign was one of great constitutional change and political reform. He had 10 illegitimate children by his mistress, Dorothea Jordan. He later married Princess Adelaide of Saxe-Meiningen, but they had no children.

'SILLY BILLY'

William joined the navy at 13 and quickly rose to the rank of captain. He had a forthright manner and was prone to making tactless remarks, which earned him the nickname 'Silly Billy', particularly with regard to his sometimes inept but nevertheless enthusiastic attempts at government. To be fair, however, he was likeable and lacked his brother's extravagances, which endeared him to the people.

DOROTHEA JORDAN

William lived with his mistress Dorothea Jordan, an actress, almost as man and wife for 21 years. She bore him 10 illegitimate children. Financial pressures forced him to marry Adelaide of Saxe-Meiningen in 1818. Whether he continued his affair with Dorothea is not known.

FACTORY ACT

Until the Factory Act was passed in 1833 (which reduced the working week to 60 hours and prohibited children under the age of 9 from working) conditions in the factories were appalling. Until then, children as young as five could be set to work and the average working day was 14 hours, including Saturdays.

SLAVERY ABOLISHED

After years of campaigning by such people as William Wilberforce, slavery was finally abolished throughout the Empire in 1833. The law met with a great deal of opposition, particularly in the colonies, where rich landowners relied heavily on slave labour. Slaves were captured from the poorer regions of the world, such as Africa, and transported to the colonies, where they became the property of rich landowners. A slave purchased for as little as £3 in Africa might fetch £24 at auction in America.

1830	1831	parliamentary system and	1833	1833
George's brother accedes to the throne as William IV.	*New London Bridge opened.*	*extend votes to further ½ million people.*	*The 'Royal William' becomes first steamship to cross Atlantic under its own power.*	*Factory Act improves hours and working conditions of women and children.*
1830	**1832**	**1833**		**1834**
'Rocket' runs on Liverpool - Manchester railway.	*First Reform Act passed to reform*	*Slavery is finally abolished throughout the British Empire.*		*Poor Law creates*

 ARCHITECTURE   📖 ARTS & LITERATURE   ⮎ EXPLORATION   💥 FAMOUS BATTLES

TOLPUDDLE MARTYRS

In 1834 six villagers from Tolpuddle, in Dorset, were arrested for joining a trade union, which at that time was still illegal. A march was organised by many who supported the six and a petition presented to the king, but to no avail. The villagers were tried and sentenced to seven years' hard labour in Australia, although they were afterwards allowed to return.

POOR LAW

In 1834 the Poor Law was passed which took the responsibility of caring for the poor away from the parishes in which they lived. The new law provided workhouses in which the poor and homeless could receive food and lodging in return for giving a day's labour. Conditions were harsh and the rewards low, but it did succeed in reducing the number of homeless beggars who slept rough on the street. Many of the poor, who had lost their jobs on the land, were forced to seek work in the crowded and dirty industrial towns.

PARLIAMENT BURNS DOWN

Parliament formerly met in part of the old royal palace of Westminster given to the Commons by Edward VI. The building burned down in a disastrous fire in 1834. The present Houses of Parliament were completed in 1867 to designs by Pugin and Barry.

FIRST REFORM ACT

William's reign saw a number of important legal and political reforms including, in 1832, the First Reform Act, which attempted to reform the voting system. The vote was extended to property owners, land owners and some tenants, and a fairer, more proportional system of allocating parliamentary seats was introduced.

MUNICIPAL REFORM ACT

The Municipal Reform Act, passed in 1835, brought political reforms to local government. It required the members of town councils to be elected by ratepayers and not by the businessmen of a town. It also made councils accountable by ordering them to publish details of their financial dealings.

REGISTRATION ACT

With the burgeoning population caused by the Industrial Revolution and the massive population movements it caused from country to town, it was decided that a greater check was needed on the people of Britain. In 1836 the registration of all births, marriages and deaths became compulsory by law.

workhouses for the poor.
1834
Tolpuddle Martyrs transported to Australia for their efforts to form a trade union

which was illegal.
1834
Palace of Westminster (Houses of Parliament) virtually destroyed by fire.

1835
Screw propeller invented, independently, in both Britain and America.
1835
Municipal Reform Act

passed making it compulsory to elect town councils and publish accounts of public records.
1836
Registration of births,

marriages and deaths made compulsory.
1837
Colour printing invented.
1837
William IV dies.

📖 GOVERNMENT   ⚕ HEALTH & MEDICINE   ⚖ JUSTICE   ✝ RELIGION   📖 SCIENCE

📖 CHARLES DICKENS (1812-70)

Charles Dickens was the greatest and most popular novelist of his day and even today his works are seldom out of print. He became a spokesman for his time with his graphic descriptions of Victorian England. All of his books were serialised, making them available to all classes. He spent the last years of his life at Gad's Hill Place, Higham, in Kent, and died there while working on his last, unfinished novel, 'The Mystery of Edwin Drood'.

📜 PEOPLE'S CHARTER

Soon into Victoria's reign, the People's Charter was issued in 1838 by a group of political reformers known as the Chartists. Its main clauses called for the right to vote for everyone, the right for anyone to seek election, secret ballots and equal representation, among others. Although not fully realised until 1944, it forms the basis of our modern parliamentary system.

🐄 SMALLPOX VACCINATION

A number of deadly diseases were prevalent in Victorian Britain, one of the worst and most contagious of which was smallpox. Several doctors, including Edward Jenner, carried out pioneering work in developing vaccines to control the spread of such diseases, though many people were afraid to take them. So, in 1853, a law was passed which made vaccination against smallpox compulsory, as part of the government's policy of health and social reforms.

BOER WAR

Between 1899 -1902 a war was fought between Britain and a group of Dutch settlers in South Africa, known as the Boers. A massive army was sent against the Boers, but it proved largely ineffective against the settlers' guerrilla tactics. Peace was eventually reached in 1902, after much loss of life on both sides.

PRINCE ALBERT

Victoria married Prince Albert of Saxe-Coburg-Gotha in 1840 and together they had nine children. It was truly a love match and they were a devoted couple. Albert was intelligent and talented and proved to be an able administrator. He designed the royal houses of Osborne (on the Isle of Wight) and Balmoral (in the Scottish Highlands) and also instigated the Great Exhibition, believing that by promoting industry it would generate more work and so help the poor. Proceeds from the profits were used to fund various public institutes, including many of London's museums. When he died, prematurely, in 1861 at the age of 42 from typhoid, the queen went into mourning for 13 years and had a number of buildings and monuments, including the Albert Hall, erected in his honour.

1837	1840	1841	1846	1852
Victoria succeeds her uncle to the throne.	*Victoria marries Albert of Saxe-Coburg-Gotha.*	*Sir Robert Peel becomes Prime Minister.*	*Corn Laws repealed.*	*Duke of Wellington dies.*
1838	**1840**	**1845/48**	**1851**	**1854/56**
People's Charter issued for political reform.	*Penny postal service introduced.*	*Potato Famine in Ireland.*	*Great Exhibition in London initiated by Prince Albert.*	*Crimean War between Britain (and France) against Russia.*

 ARCHITECTURE   ARTS & LITERATURE    EXPLORATION   💧 FAMOUS BATTLES

VICTORIA

BORN 1819 • ACCEDED 1837 • DIED 1901

Victoria came to the throne at the age of 18 after her uncle, William IV, died childless in 1837. She was destined to become our longest reigning monarch and ruler of the greatest empire the world has ever seen. She came to the throne with enthusiasm and consulted frequently with her ministers. Some of our greatest prime ministers came to power during her long reign, including Lord Melbourne, Sir Robert Peel, Gladstone and Disraeli.

GREAT EXHIBITION

The Great Exhibition of 1851 was the brainchild of Prince Albert. Britain was known as the 'workshop of the world' and the exhibition was intended as a shop window, an outward display of the country's achievements. It was a runaway success and attracted over six million visitors. It was held in the purpose-built Crystal Palace, a masterpiece of glass and cast iron, designed by Joseph Paxton. The building covered over 26 acres and was moved from its site in Hyde Park to Sydenham after the exhibition, but sadly burned down in 1936.

PENNY POST SERVICE

Although private postal services had been in operation since at least Tudor times, no national postal system existed until 1840 when the Penny Post was introduced. This revolutionised the delivery of letters when, for the small payment of 1d. (0.4p) a letter could be sent anywhere in the country. The first stamp issued was the Penny Black and the very next day John Tomlinson became the world's first stamp collector.

IRISH POTATO FAMINE

Many of the people of Ireland lived at subsistence level, surviving on a meagre diet, mostly consisting of potatoes. When a serious blight hit the potato crop in 1845 many died of starvation. Between 1845-49 about 1.3 million people died, while about the same number emigrated in an effort to find a better life.

CRIMEAN WAR

The Crimean War was fought between Britain and Russia (1854-56) on a peninsula that is now part of modern-day Turkey. The 'Charge of the Light Brigade' took place during this war at the Battle of Balaclava in 1854. It was one of Britain's worst military disasters, resulting in the deaths or serious wounding of nearly half of the cavalrymen of the Light Brigade. Casualties in the war were high with many of the injured being cared for by Florence Nightingale and her team of nurses.

1856 *Victoria Cross first introduced for bravery in wartime.* **1857** *Indian Mutiny against*	*British rule.* **1867** *Canada declared first country within the British Empire to become an independent dominion.*	**1869** *Irish Church is disestablished.* **1870** *Education becomes compulsory for all children.*	**1872** *Secret voting introduced at elections.* **1876** *Victoria becomes Empress of India.*	**1889/1902** *Boer War breaks out in South Africa.* **1901** *Victoria dies; our longest reigning monarch.*

GOVERNMENT   HEALTH & MEDICINE   JUSTICE   RELIGION   SCIENCE

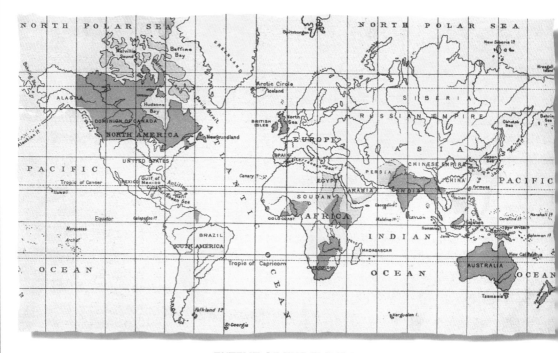

EXTENT OF THE EMPIRE

This map shows the full extent of the Empire. All of the countries under British control are coloured orange.
They included such distant lands as Canada, Australia, New Zealand, India, parts of Indonesia and the Far East,
large tracts of Africa and several islands in the southern oceans, used as convenient outposts and trading posts for
the merchant fleets of the Empire. As a direct result of the Empire, the English language is now the most widespread
and commonly spoken language in the world.

LARGEST EMPIRE EVER KNOWN

Because it was not conceived as a single plan, the British Empire grew very slowly, allowing new colonies to be consolidated and gradually brought under British control. At its beginnings in the 16th century it consisted only of a handful of settlements in North America and grew hardly at all during the 17th century. Under the Georges, the boundaries were stretched further, coming to the full height of its power under Victoria. At its greatest extent the Empire covered one quarter of the land mass of the world; the largest empire ever known.

THE COMMONWEALTH

In many respects, a large part of the British Empire still exists, known today as the Commonwealth. Although few countries take kindly to being governed by strangers, and Britain ruthlessly exploited the riches of countries under its control, many prospered under British rule. The British way of life was spread round the world and many of the advantages of modern civilisation were shared with less well-off countries. Initially, attempts at independence were stoutly resisted, but gradually all of the Empire's member states received their independence, most without resorting to violence, and most countries retain friendly relations with Britain, earning a respect no other empire can claim.

ARCHITECTURE   ARTS & LITERATURE   EXPLORATION   FAMOUS BATTLES

THE BRITISH EMPIRE

he expansion of the British Empire had more to do with trade and the wealth it generated than with world domination as a super power, which is possibly why it was so successful. Although obviously aided by the military, it was not itself militarily-led. Unlike other great empires, such as the Romans, who conquered other lands, the British Empire concentrated more on controlling the economy and ultimately the government of other countries. Also, unlike other empires, its dominions were acquired in a piecemeal fashion at different times, stretching in an ad hoc fashion across the globe, instead of following a coherent pattern radiating out from its imperial centre.

VICTORIA-EMPRESS OF INDIA

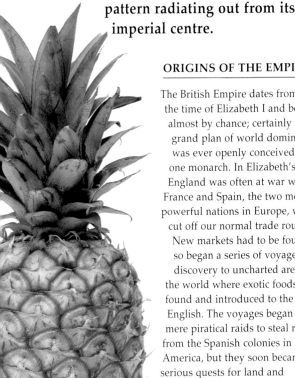

ORIGINS OF THE EMPIRE

The British Empire dates from the time of Elizabeth I and began almost by chance; certainly no grand plan of world domination was ever openly conceived by any one monarch. In Elizabeth's time, England was often at war with France and Spain, the two most powerful nations in Europe, which cut off our normal trade routes. New markets had to be found and so began a series of voyages of discovery to uncharted areas of the world where exotic foods were found and introduced to the English. The voyages began as mere piratical raids to steal riches from the Spanish colonies in South America, but they soon became serious quests for land and dominions, mostly along the eastern coast of North America.

While many of the lands taken over by Britain were relatively unsophisticated before our arrival, India was, by contrast, a land of great antiquity, with a rich cultural history. Britain's original settlements there were minimal and controlled by a commercial company, the East India Company, with protection by the British army. Following a mutiny in 1857-58, however, Britain assumed full control of India. Queen Victoria was created Empress of India, and all subsequent kings became Emperor until India was granted independence in 1947.

DECLINE OF THE EMPIRE

The Empire probably reached its zenith and fullest extent in terms of both land mass and power at about 1920 when the former German colonies in Africa and Asia were taken over following the First World War. Eventually, resources were stretched too thinly for successful control of so large an empire. The military were unable to sustain the growth and when several countries expressed a wish to re-assert their own sovereignty, coupled with serious economic problems at home, the Empire began to break up and fall into decline.

GOVERNMENT   HEALTH & MEDICINE   JUSTICE   RELIGION   SCIENCE

EDWARD VII

BORN 1841 • ACCEDED 1901 • DIED 1910

dward VII was the eldest son of Queen Victoria and Prince Albert, though his relationship with his parents, especially his mother, was often strained. Even though he took over many of her administrative duties as Prince of Wales, she did not entirely trust his judgement and often excluded him from any real involvement in governmental matters. He lived life to the full (which earned him both popularity and derision) and had several mistresses, even though he was said to be happily married to Princess Alexandra, of Denmark, for many years.

SANDRINGHAM

The Norfolk estate of Sandringham has become a great, out-of-town favourite as a royal residence. It was purchased by Edward VII while he was still Prince of Wales in 1862 as a private residence. It consisted then of a large, neglected house and over 6,000 acres of land. Edward extended and improved the property considerably over the years and it is now often the centre of Christmas celebrations for the present royal family.

AUSTRALIA

Australia was granted dominion status in 1901, its people having long expressed a wish to be self-governing. Australia, although lightly populated by aboriginal natives, was largely an empty wilderness when it was added to the British Empire. Many new settlers were encouraged to move there to establish a proper, self-sufficient colony. Also, to help boost the population, many prisoners in England had their sentences commuted to transportation to the colonies, especially Australia.

THE BEGINNINGS OF THE WELFARE STATE

In 1887 the Independent Labour Party was founded, with the express intent of social reform, particularly for the downtrodden working

classes. Although they did not form their first government until 1924, they greatly influenced the other political parties, especially the Liberals, and pressed for several measures to eradicate social evils. Between 1906-09 a number of reforms were introduced, including labour exchanges for the unemployed and free school meals for the poor. Old-age pensions were introduced in 1908 for all people over 70.

1901	1901	1902	1903	1904
Edward VII accedes to the throne.	*Marconi makes first trans-Atlantic radio transmission.*	*Robert Bosch invents the spark plug.*	*Emmeline Pankhurst founds the Women's Social and Political Union (known as the Suffragettes).*	*First escalator opens in Paris.*
1901	**1902**	**1903**		**1904**
Australia granted dominion status within the Empire.	*Order of Merit introduced.*	*The Wright brothers make the first manned flight.*		*Britain and France sign the Entente Cordiale.*

 ARCHITECTURE   ARTS & LITERATURE   EXPLORATION   FAMOUS BATTLES

EMMELINE PANKHURST

In 1903 Emmeline Pankhurst formed the Women's Social and Political Union (WSPU) to fight for women's rights.

The crusade for women's rights had been in existence for some time and had won some victories, but in 1903 women were still not allowed to vote. Members of WSPU were known as 'suffragettes' and in 1908 over half a million women gathered at a rally in Hyde Park, known as Women's Sunday, to protest at the inequality of women's rights. Suffragettes, including Emmeline Pankhurst, were often arrested for demonstrating, eventually winning their rights in 1918, when all women over 30 were given the right to vote, extended in 1928 to all women over 21.

INDISCRETIONS

Edward spent so long in the wings waiting to be king that he spent most of his time socialising, enjoying the pomp and the ceremony that accompanies the crown. He was quite open about his many affairs and had liaisons with Lillie Langtry (right) and Sarah Bernhardt, both famous actresses of the time.

WRIGHT BROTHERS

The first powered flight in a 'heavier-than-air machine' (as opposed to balloon flight) was by the Americans Orville and Wilbur Wright in December 1903. Their biplane (called 'The Flier') took off from Kitty Hawk, in North Carolina, and was based on unpowered gliders developed by the German Otto Lilienthal some 10 years before.

ENTENTE CORDIALE

The historic 'Entente Cordiale' (or 'cordial understanding') was an agreement between Britain and France to settle territorial disputes, further extended in 1908 to include Russia ('the Triple Entente'). Edward had a great love of France and on a visit to Paris in 1903 he paved the way for the political discussions that followed. The major powers of Europe seemed to be on a collision course and the agreement was intended to settle land disputes and avert war by forming an opposing group to balance the power of the Triple Alliance between Germany, Italy and Austria-Hungary.

1905	1907	1908	(as Chancellor) introduces	English Channel.
First dial telephone invented.	New Zealand	Triple Entente signed	the controversial	1910
1905	granted dominion status.	between Britain, France	'People's Budget'.	Parliament curbs the power
Completion of the	1908	and Russia.	1909	of the House of Lords.
electrification of London's	Henry Ford introduced	1909	Louis Blériot flies single-	1910
underground.	the Model-T car.	Lloyd-George	winged aircraft across	Edward VII dies.

GOVERNMENT   HEALTH & MEDICINE   JUSTICE   RELIGION   SCIENCE

The Hanoverians

GEORGE V

BORN 1865 • ACCEDED 1910 •DIED 1936

As has so often been the case with the British monarchy, George V was not born to be king and only acceded to the throne because of the death of his brother, Edward. His reign was one of great turbulence, marked by social unrest, a world war and changes to the constitution that curbed the powers of the House of Lords. George V made the first Christmas broadcast to the nation to try to lift the people's spirits, a tradition still performed by the ruling monarch today.

RUSSIAN REVOLUTION

George V's cousin was Nicholas II, Tsar of Russia. Revolution broke out in Russia in 1917, resulting in the abdication of the Tsar, who, along with his family, was murdered soon afterwards by the Bolsheviks. The story of the revolution is a complex one. It began in 1905 following a disastrous war between Russia and Japan. The Tsar agreed to certain concessions and peace prevailed, but when these were withdrawn in 1917, revolution erupted again. The Tsar was forced to abdicate and a western-style liberal republican government was formed, but this was itself overthrown eight months later by the Bolsheviks, a socialist group led by Lenin. The revolution itself had been comparatively bloodless, but the civil war that ensued between the counter-revolutionary 'white' Russians and the 'red' Russians led by Trotsky led to an estimated six million Russians losing their lives.

TITANIC SINKS

In April 1912 the 'SS Titanic' set sail on her maiden voyage from Britain to America. The ship was then the biggest ever built and was claimed to be unsinkable. It struck an iceberg in bad weather a few days later and sank within hours. Because insufficient lifeboats were provided, 1513 of the original 2224 passengers drowned. The wreck was discovered in 1980 and subsequently explored and photographed. An exhibition was mounted at the National Maritime Museum in Greenwich in 1995 of artefacts retrieved from the wreck.

1910 George V accedes to the throne. **1911** Parliament Act issued. **1911** National Insurance	Act provides financial benefits for the sick and unemployed. **1912** The Titanic sinks on her maiden voyage.	**1914** The church in Wales is disestablished. **1914** The 1st World War breaks out.	**1914** Battle of Ypres **1915** Gallipoli expedition fails. **1916** Battle of the Somme	**1916** David Lloyd George becomes Prime Minister. **1917** Russian Revolution breaks out.

 ARCHITECTURE  ARTS & LITERATURE  EXPLORATION   FAMOUS BATTLES

GENERAL STRIKE

In May 1926 Britain was subjected to a General Strike. It had been caused by a growing crisis in the mining industry. When miners were asked to work longer hours for less money, they came out on strike, supported by an estimated 90% of all workers in Britain, bringing the country to a virtual standstill. The government had anticipated the strike and instigated various interim measures, including use of the military for essential services. The Trades Union Congress (TUC) negotiated a return to work after just nine days, having failed to get their demands met. The miners felt betrayed and stayed out on strike for a further six months, until starvation forced them to accept defeat. Shown above is a policeman protecting a strike-breaking bus driver.

GREAT DEPRESSION

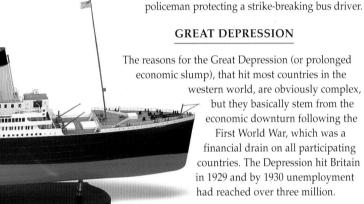

The reasons for the Great Depression (or prolonged economic slump), that hit most countries in the western world, are obviously complex, but they basically stem from the economic downturn following the First World War, which was a financial drain on all participating countries. The Depression hit Britain in 1929 and by 1930 unemployment had reached over three million.

IRELAND DIVIDED

Protestant English settlers moved to Ireland in Tudor times, particularly around the Ulster area. The Irish Parliament came to be dominated by Protestants and the Catholics, who were the majority, became second class citizens. In 1920-22 failure to resolve the problems in Ireland resulted in an agreement to partition the country. The six counties of Ulster became the province of Northern Ireland and remained part of the United Kingdom, while the remaining counties became known as Eire, the Free State of Ireland.

LLOYD GEORGE

David Lloyd George (First Earl of Dwyfor, 1863-1945) was one of the great orators of his time. Liberal M.P. for Caernarvon Boroughs between 1890-1945, he became Prime Minister of a coalition government between 1916-22.

🥣 NATIONAL HEALTH INSURANCE ACT

The National Insurance Act was passed in 1911 by Herbert Asquith's Liberal government, which gave manual workers and many other employees a small wage and free medical attention during periods of sickness. A small weekly insurance premium was collected from each worker, which was supplemented by the government. The Act, which also provided certain workers with unemployment pay and was extended in 1920 to most other workers, still forms the basis of the modern welfare state.

📜 REFORM ACT

The Reform Act of 1918 finally gave the vote to certain women over the age of 30 after years of campaigning by the suffragette movement. During World War I many jobs normally done by men had to be performed by women which, indirectly, helped the suffragette cause.

📜 STATUTE OF WESTMINSTER

By George V's reign several countries in the British Empire, including Canada, Australia and New Zealand, had received dominion status and in 1931 their independence was recognised by the Statute of Westminster. Although still part of the British Commonwealth and influenced by Britain, such countries became self-governing.

1918	1919	1920/21	1928	1932
1st World War ends.	Lady Astor becomes first	Ireland partitioned.	Right to vote	First Christmas
1918	woman M.P. in Britain.	**1926**	given to all	speech by the
Reform Act	**1919**	General Strike	women over 21.	reigning monarch.
gives votes to	Alcock and Brown fly non-	in support	**1931**	**1936**
women over 30.	stop across the Atlantic.	of coal miners.	Great Depression.	George V dies.

🏛 GOVERNMENT   🥣 HEALTH & MEDICINE   ⚖ JUSTICE   ✝ RELIGION   📗 SCIENCE

WORLD WAR I
(1914-1918)

*T*he underlying causes of the First World War are, even now, little understood in their entirety. Contrary to popular belief, it is unlikely that Germany was at that time making a bid for world domination. It began more as a trade war between the various powers of Europe who all had colonies scattered around the world. Each country mistrusted the others and a series of alliances were drawn up to spread the balance of power and prevent any one country from becoming too powerful. What started out with Germany flexing its muscles to protect its dominions and bullying its near neighbours into submission, soon escalated into first, Europe-wide, and then world-wide warfare.

THE KAISER (1859-1941)

The Kaiser, Wilhelm II, was Queen Victoria's grandson and George V's cousin, though George fully supported the government's stand against the Germans when they invaded Belgium in 1914. Wilhelm was German Emperor and King of Prussia between 1888-1918. He was forced to abdicate after the war and fled to the Netherlands in exile until his death.

THE WAR BEGINS

The spark that began the conflict occurred in 1914 when the heir to the Austrian throne, Archduke Franz Ferdinand, was assassinated. The Austrians blamed the Serbians and declared war on them. Russia rushed to Serbia's aid and Germany to Austria's. Britain became involved when Germany invaded Belgium, which had been neutral until then, posing a threat to Britain's maritime security.

TRENCH WARFARE

Trench warfare, a comparatively new innovation, dominated the military strategies of the First World War. The digging of trenches by sappers and miners had long been known in siege operations, but here it became the dominant strategy following the deadlock after the Battle of Ypres. Thousands of soldiers were forced to live in the trenches, drawn up by each side along the battle lines, often for months at a time. Conditions were appalling and the loss of life was horrendous as periodically one side or the other would rush the trenches of the enemy to gain a few yards of territory.

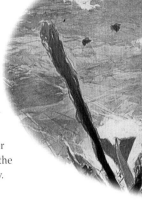

ARCHITECTURE   ARTS & LITERATURE   EXPLORATION   FAMOUS BATTLES

JOIN TOGETHER
TRAIN TOGETHER
EMBARK TOGETHER
FIGHT TOGETHER

LIEUT. JACKA V.C

Enlist in the Sportsmen's Thousand

SHOW THE ENEMY WHAT
AUSTRALIAN SPORTING MEN CAN DO.

VOLUNTEERS SIGN UP

The allied army consisted largely of untrained civilians. Mounting unemployment at home meant that there was no shortage of volunteers to sign up for military service in Europe. Creative advertisements were used to encourage young men in particular to join up. The average age of recruits was just 19. The conflict was said to be the war to end all wars and was expected to be over in just six weeks.

PEACE TREATY

Following the German defeat in the Marne, the Kaiser left Germany for Holland. Germany formally surrendered on 11th November 1918 and signed armistice agreements dictated by the allies, marking the end of what was probably the bloodiest and most titanic conflict ever fought. Germany was disarmed and forbidden to re-arm, in addition to being presented with a huge bill for war damage, but later ignored both of these terms. The Peace Treaty of Versailles (below) in 1919 (and others) redrew the map of the world, dividing up the German colonies and the old Austro-Hungarian Empire among the allies. Several entirely new European states were thus created and a League of Nations formed to prevent such a war happening again.

DOG FIGHT

A new form of warfare emerged in the First World War, that of attack from the air. Britain suffered 52 air raids between 1914-18, killing over 500 people. Bombs were dropped mostly from huge gas filled airships, protected by fighter planes. By the end of the war Britain had the largest air force in the world. One-to-one 'dog-fights' become a common occurrence.

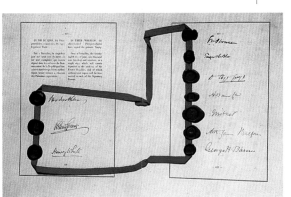

GOVERNMENT　　HEALTH & MEDICINE　　JUSTICE　　RELIGION　　SCIENCE

ILLUSTRAZIONE DEL POPOLO

POPULAR PRINCE

As Prince of Wales, Edward was popular with the people. He visited America on several occasions. He was happiest when socialising and disliked the pomp and ceremony that accompanied royal occasions, which endeared him to the people, but infuriated his father.

MRS. SIMPSON

Mrs. Wallis Warfield Simpson was an American, who had already divorced one husband and was in the process of divorcing her second, when she met Prince Edward in 1931. The two soon fell in love, sparking off a constitutional crisis. At that time the Church of England refused to bless the marriage of divorcees, which made her an unsuitable candidate for a queen. Once King, Edward would also be head of the English Church, which made the dilemma more than just a personal problem.

SPANISH CIVIL WAR

In 1923 a military coup by Miguel Rivera and the Spanish Nationalists ousted the democratic government of Spain, assisted by the fascist states of Italy and Nazi Germany. Between 1930-31 Rivera's government was itself overthrown by Republicans, who won the general election in 1936. Civil war broke out the same year between the Republicans and the Nationalists, under General Franco. The civil war came to an end in 1939 with General Franco being declared dictator, a position he held until his death in 1975. In that year, King Juan Carlos I became the new head of state, followed two years later by the first free elections since 1936.

CRYSTAL PALACE BURNS DOWN

Joseph Paxton's masterpiece in glass and iron, the Crystal Palace, accidentally burned down in 1936. This incredible building had been erected in Hyde Park in 1851 for the Great Exhibition and had already survived a move to Sydenham, in south London, when it was carefully dismantled and re-erected at its new site. Parts of the building had been let out and it is believed a spark from electrical equipment ignited the accumulated dust in the cellars and set fire to the building. The blaze, which quickly took hold, could be seen for miles around.

FIRST TELEVISION BROADCAST

Television is a direct extension of radio and was pioneered by the Scottish inventor John Logie Baird. He first demonstrated the use of television broadcasts in 1925. The first television service in the world was broadcast by the B.B.C. in 1936, though it was another 30 years before television became a common feature in most households.

1936	1936	Britain re-arms in	1936	1936
Edward VIII accedes to the throne.	*Spanish Civil War breaks out.*	*preparation for another war.*	*The Supermarine Spitfire makes its maiden flight.*	*First train ferry service across English Channel.*
1936	**1936**	**1936**	**1936**	*English Channel.*
Jean Batten flies solo from Britain to New Zealand.	*Hitler rebuilds the German armed forces and*	*The Crystal Palace burns down.*	*First television service in the world by the B.B.C.*	**1936**
				Edward VIII abdicates.

🏛 ARCHITECTURE   📖 ARTS & LITERATURE   ⚑ EXPLORATION   ✸ FAMOUS BATTLES

EDWARD VIII

BORN 1894 • ACCEDED 1936 • ABDICATED 1936 • DIED 1972

dward VIII acceded to the throne on 29th January 1936, but ruled for just 325 days, abdicating the throne on 11th December later the same year. He was created Duke of Windsor soon after his abdication, a title he held until his death, in self-imposed exile in France, in 1972. His relationship with his father, George V, had always been strained. George is reported to have said that Edward would ruin himself within a year of succeeding to the throne, little realising the prophetic truth of his statement.

OUTSPOKEN VIEWS

Edward was noted for being somewhat headstrong and for holding outspoken and sometimes controversial views. On one occasion, while visiting Wales as king (one of his few public engagements) he embarrassed the government by saying that something should be done to reduce unemployment and he even contributed towards the miners' relief fund during the General Strike. He is also known to have held certain sympathies with Germany during World War Two.

EXILE IN FRANCE

Edward's decision to abdicate, although received with sympathy by the general population, met with grave disapproval by members of the royal family, many of whom disowned him and refused to acknowledge Mrs. Simpson. Edward waited until after his brother Albert's coronation as George VI the following year before he married. The wedding ceremony was held at Chateau de Cande, near Tours, in France, on 3rd June 1937. They withdrew completely from public life and Edward died in exile on 18th May 1972.

THE KING ABDICATES

The Prime Minister, Stanley Baldwin, made the government's position crystal clear. Neither the monarchy nor the Church could be brought into disrepute and so Edward had to choose between the crown and Mrs. Simpson. The King decided that he did not want to continue ruling without Wallis as his queen and so chose to abdicate the crown. He did so on 11th December 1936, before he had been crowned. A formal 'Instrument of Abdication' was drawn up by Baldwin, which was rushed through Parliament. The following day Edward spoke to the public on the radio as a private citizen, giving the heartfelt reasons for his decision.

L'illustré du Petit Journal

Le duc de WINDSOR et Mrs WARFIELD vivent dans le château de Candé leurs derniers jours de fiançailles avant la célébration de leur mariage

GOVERNMENT   HEALTH & MEDICINE   JUSTICE   RELIGION   SCIENCE

GEORGE VI

BORN 1895 • ACCEDED 1936 • DIED 1952

When Edward VIII abdicated in 1936 the crown passed to George V's second son, Albert, who assumed the name George VI on his coronation. Another monarch not groomed for kingship, he was an intensely shy man, nervous in public, and suffered from an acute stammer. He is said to have confessed to his cousin, Lord Louis Mountbatten, 'I never wanted this to happen. I'm only a naval officer, it's the only thing I know about'. Nevertheless, George proved himself more than equal to the task, especially during the War years.

LADY ELIZABETH BOWES-LYON

George married Lady Elizabeth Bowes-Lyon in 1923 and together they had two daughters. A devoted wife and mother, Elizabeth soon became a firm royal favourite with the British public. When George died unexpectedly at the comparatively young age of 56, she continued to offer her support to the young Queen Elizabeth II and she still carries out several public duties each year, despite her age.

FAMILY MAN

George became one of our most popular monarchs, due in no small part to his lack of pretension. Aware of his own shortcomings, he strove hard to overcome his stammer so that he could perform his duties with dignity. Always a very private, family man, he moved his family into the Royal Lodge in the grounds of Windsor Castle. This, coupled with his decision to remain in Britain throughout the War, endeared him to the public.

VISITING THE TROOPS

George refused to leave England during the 2nd World War, even after Buckingham Palace was bombed in 1940, and made several morale-boosting visits to the troops abroad. He also wanted to take a more active role in the war effort, though he was dissuaded from doing so by Winston Churchill, the Prime Minister. He instigated the George Cross and the George Medal, awarded to recognise civilian heroism. In 1942 the George Cross was awarded to the entire population of Malta in recognition of their brave resistance to a massive German onslaught.

INDIA GIVEN INDEPENDENCE

Most of the member states of the Empire sent troops to help with Britain's war effort. When the war was over, one of the principal effects was to strengthen the resolve of nationalism within the Empire, especially in the Near and Far East, where a bitter struggle for independence had been going on for some years. Supported by the new Labour government, legislation was passed in 1947 to give Burma, India, Pakistan and Ceylon independence, making them self-governing dominions of the British Commonwealth. Here we can see Gandhi being arrested in 1932 for his civil disobedience tactic.

1936 Edward's younger brother Albert accedes to the throne as George VI.	**1940** The 'Mallard' sets all-time speed record for steam train at 126 m.p.h. **1939** 2nd World War	breaks out. **1940** Dunkirk - evacuation of allied troops from beaches' of northern France.	**1940** Winston Churchill becomes Prime Minister. **1940** Battle of Britain fought in skies over southern	England, German defeat halts invasion of Britain. **1941** U.S.A. enters war following Japanese bombing of Pearl Harbour.

🏛 ARCHITECTURE   📖 ARTS & LITERATURE   🏳 EXPLORATION   💣 FAMOUS BATTLES

FESTIVAL OF BRITAIN

In the years after the Second World War the government, with the full support of George, decided to hold a huge festival to boost morale and give the people hope for a brighter future. The Festival of Britain was held in 1951, on the centenary of the Great Exhibition of 1851. Concentrating on Britain's artistic achievements, the festival was a great success and included the building of the Festival Hall on the Embankment.

CORONATION MUG

Since the 18th century it has been fashionable for china and porcelain manufacturers to produce commemorative pieces to celebrate significant royal occasions, such as coronations, weddings and jubilees. They have since become collectors' pieces. This decorative mug was produced to mark the coronation of George VI in May 1937.

🥄 NATIONAL HEALTH SERVICE

When the Second World War ended a growing wish for social change swept the country. Many people were tired of the old ways and wanted something new. The Labour Party won a sensational victory in the 1945 election and within three years radical social changes were introduced. Between 1946-48 the National Insurance, Assistance and Health Service Acts were passed which provided for a free health service for all, based on equality rather than on an ability to pay. Sickness, unemployment and pension payments were also significantly revised and several key, but ailing industries, such as the railways, gas and electric companies, were nationalised.

📖 UNITED NATIONS FORMED

The United Nations was formed in 1945 immediately after the end of the Second World War. The original Charter was drawn up by the Allied Powers to preserve world peace and security, to encourage nations to be just towards one another, to help nations co-operate in solving their problems and to act as an agency through which all nations could work together to achieve these goals. The General Assembly of the United Nations meets annually in New York.

LA DOMENICA DEL CORRIERE

1942	1945	1947	1949	1951
Kodak introduces colour print film.	End of 2nd World War.	India partitioned and granted independence.	Boeing Superfortress makes first non-stop flight around the world.	Winston Churchill becomes Prime Minster again.
1944	1945	1948	1951	1952
D-Day landings in Normandy.	United Nations founded to promote world peace.	National Health Service formed.	Festival of Britain.	George VI dies.

📖 GOVERNMENT   🥄 HEALTH & MEDICINE   ⚖ JUSTICE   ✝ RELIGION   📖 SCIENCE

WINSTON CHURCHILL
(1874-1965)

Probably the greatest wartime leader this country has ever seen, Sir Winston Churchill was born at Blenheim Palace in 1874. He began his somewhat chequered career as a newspaper correspondent during the Boer War. He became a Conservative M.P. in 1900, joined the Liberals in 1904 and changed back to the Tories in 1929. When Neville Chamberlain resigned in 1940 he became the Prime Minister of a coalition government for the remainder of the War and again between 1951-55 as a Conservative. Also a writer and painter of some repute, he won the Nobel Prize for Literature in 1953.

WORLD WAR II
(1939-1945)

*H*he reasons for the outbreak of the Second World War are much easier to understand than those for the First World War and grew directly, as a natural consequence, from the first world conflict. Following that war the blight of economic recession fell upon the whole of Europe. It affected Germany harder because it had been presented with a massive compensation bill to cover the cost of repairing the damage of war. Unemployment and inflation ran unchecked and the resulting sense of grievance paved the way for social unrest. When the fanatical Adolf Hitler appeared on the scene, inciting the people with his powerful speeches of world domination, they willingly followed. Having already flouted the Treaty of Versailles by building up the German army, when he invaded Poland on 1st September 1939 Britain and France, as her allies, were drawn into events. War was declared on Germany on 3rd September 1939.

D-DAY LANDINGS

At dawn on 6th June 1944 the Allies began their decisive push back against the Germans, beginning with the invasion of France. The Germans had built a chain of fortifications along the Channel shore and made all the ports impregnable from attack. On that day a series of landings began on the beaches of Normandy, known as 'Operation Overlord'. Altogether some 5000 ships carried over 300,000 men, 54,000 vehicles and 100,000 tons of supplies to France, protected by 10,000 warplanes. What made the invasion possible was a British invention called 'Mulberries', or floating harbours, which enabled the Allies to bypass the German-held Channel ports.

END OF HOSTILITIES

At the end of World War I over 10 million people had been killed, most of them military personnel. The final death toll after hostilities ended in World War II was much higher because of civilian casualties, and exceeded 40 million. The war in Europe ended on 8th May 1945 when Germany surrendered unconditionally. The war dragged on in the Pacific a little longer because Japan refused to give up the fight. In August, however, America dropped two atomic bombs on Japanese cities, causing unprecedented damage. On 14th August Japan also surrendered. The Second World War was over.

🏛 ARCHITECTURE   📖 ARTS & LITERATURE   🏳 EXPLORATION   🔥 FAMOUS BATTLES

PRINCESS ELIZABETH

During the War George VI made several morale-boosting trips abroad to visit the troops. Although only 13 when war was declared, the young Princess Elizabeth continued her father's personal involvement in the war effort by signing up with the Auxiliary Transport Service on her 18th birthday, which won great public acclaim.

DUNKIRK

After just eight months of the war Hitler's superior army (in terms of both size and equipment) swept across northern Europe, cutting off the allied Anglo-French-Belgian forces. The Belgians surrendered, leaving the French and British hemmed in around the Channel port of Dunkirk. What followed was little short of a miracle. Under heavy cloud cover, which protected them from aerial attack, a convoy of British naval and merchant ships, supported by a flotilla of tugs, yachts, fishing boats, barges, (indeed anything that could make the journey) somehow managed to evacuate the bulk of the army (some 338,000) back to England, and safety.

WOMEN'S LAND ARMY

Unlike any other war in history, the Second World War directly affected the lives of civilians at home as much as the troops fighting on the front. Women were employed to do many of the jobs formerly done by men (who were forced to join the services) including munitions and farm work. The latter became known affectionately as the 'Women's Land Army'.

ADOLF HITLER (1889-1945)

Born in Austria, Adolf Hitler served as a corporal in the German army during World War I. He became leader of the extreme right-wing Nationalist Socialist Party (Nazi) in 1920 and three years later attempted, unsuccessfully, to overthrow the government. During his subsequent term in prison he wrote the political treatise 'Mein Kampf', in which he outlined his intentions to control Europe. On his release he returned to politics and won the parliamentary election in 1930, becoming chancellor in 1933. He is believed to have committed suicide after the fall of Berlin in 1945.

THE BATTLE OF BRITAIN

The Battle of Britain was the first major battle to be fought solely in the air. It began in July 1940 shortly after France had fallen to the Germans, when Hitler launched operation 'Sealion', the invasion of Britain. To establish air supremacy, which Hitler needed to launch his invasion plans, the German Luftwaffe fought it out with the R.A.F. over the skies of south-east England for the next two months. The supremacy of the Spitfires and Hurricanes over the German Messerschmitt 109s eventually won the battle. Losses were heavy (in August alone over 300 of the 1400 British pilots were killed) but Hitler accepted defeat and called off the invasion on 17th September.

U.S.A. ENTERS THE WAR

Japan joined forces with Germany and Italy against the allied forces of Europe. On 7th December 1941 America was brought into the conflict when the U.S. fleet was subjected to an unprovoked and quite devastating attack on the naval base at Pearl Harbour, in Hawaii.

GOVERNMENT   HEALTH & MEDICINE   JUSTICE   RELIGION   SCIENCE

⮂ SPACE TRAVEL

Towards the end of the Second World War a great deal of research was carried out on rocket development, which was later put to use in the American and Russian space programmes. The first communications satellite (Sputnik) was put into space by the Russians in 1957, followed by the first manned space flight by Yuri Gagarin in 1961. On 20th July 1969 the U.S.A. succeeded in launching the first manned space flight (Apollo 11) to land on the moon.

⬤ GULF WAR

On 2nd August 1990 the President of Iraq, Saddam Hussein, invaded neighbouring Kuwait, having failed to reach an agreement over oil prices. Days later, the U.N. imposed economic sanctions on Iraq and on 29th November they passed a resolution authorising the use of military force to liberate Kuwait. A brief, high-technology war ensued, resulting in an allied victory, headed by America and Britain. Kuwait was liberated in February 1991, followed by a ceasefire in April. A U.N. peacekeeping force was afterwards sent to Iraq.

MARGARET THATCHER

Margaret Thatcher became Britain's first woman Prime Minister in 1979 when she swept to power under the Conservative Party. Always a controversial figure, she proved also to be one of our ablest administrators and is generally regarded as lifting Britain out of recession, though her policies were often seen as overly harsh. She suffered a somewhat ignominious end to a glittering political career when, in 1990, she was ousted as head of the Conservative Party by her fellow politicians.

BRITAIN JOINS E.E.C.

The European Economic Community, now simply the European Community (E.C.), was formed in1957 by the Treaty of Rome. Known as the Common Market, it was founded in post-war Europe to provide economic security to its member states by working collectively to support one another. Britain applied for membership several times before finally being accepted in 1973.

POLL TAX REINTRODUCED

In 1989 the Conservative government of the day, under Margaret Thatcher, attempted to reintroduce the Poll Tax (known as the Community Charge) which levied a local council tax across the board, regardless of an individual's ability to pay. It met with widespread revolt from the public and many people were taken to court for non-payment. It proved as unsuccessful as the first attempt to introduce the tax in 1381, which led to the Peasants' Revolt on that occasion. The tax was withdrawn and replaced with the current Council Tax system.

1952	1953	1959	*for the first time.*	1969
Elizabeth II accedes to the throne.	*First hovercraft built in Britain.*	*Discovery of oil in the North Sea.*	1965	*First manned space flight lands on the moon.*
1953	1955	1962	*Sir Winston Churchill dies.*	1969
Edmund Hillary conquers Mount Everest.	*Churchill resigns as Prime Minister.*	*The Beatles enter the British music charts*	1969	*'Concord' makes its maiden flight.*
			Prince Charles invested as Prince of Wales.	

ELIZABETH II

BORN 1926 • ACCEDED 1952

lizabeth came to the throne at the age of 25 on the unexpected death of her father. One of only a handful of queens to rule Britain, she has become a firm favourite with the public and restored much of the popularity of the monarchy. Although her official duties are limited, she still officially presides at the state opening of Parliament and remains supreme head of the British armed services. Elizabeth married Philip Mountbatten in 1947 (who then became Duke of Edinburgh) and together they have had four children.

THE FUTURE OF THE MONARCHY

Given the present minimalist influence over affairs of state, it would seem probable that Britain will continue to preserve its monarchy. There are no great movements afoot to abolish the monarchy, though it has fallen in popularity in recent years. The Royal family is constantly in the public eye, both at home and abroad. Their charity work, family disputes and wide-varying press coverage keeps the future of the monarchy a constant topic of conversation.

THE PEOPLE'S PRINCESS

On 31st August 1997, Princess Diana (the mother of the future king - Prince William) suffered a fatal car crash on the streets of Paris. Although loosing her royal status, after her divorce from Prince Charles, she was always revered as the 'People's Princess', notably for her charitable work. Her early death sent shockwaves throughout the world and established her as a genuine world icon. Over 2.5 billion people watched her funeral - the largest television audience for a single event.

📖 THE SWINGING 60s

In the post-war years, a social revolution swept the Western world. Young people were no longer prepared to accept the values of their forefathers without question. A generation of rebels established new movements, particularly in art and music. The movement began with the new Rock and Roll music of America, but in the 1960s it was Britain that led the way. The most influential popular musical group of the time were the Beatles, still widely enjoyed today.

💣 FALKLANDS WAR

In 1982 a military junta in Argentina invaded the Falkland Islands and South Georgia, a self governing British dependency in the South Atlantic off the Argentina coast. The Argentinians seized control, even though the islands (known to them as the Islas Malvinas) had never been Argentinian territory. Britain sent a task force, headed by the largest fleet massed by this country since the Second World War. After a brief two month war Britain emerged victorious, though not without a considerable struggle.

1971	1973	1979	1989	1997
Britain adopts decimal currency.	*B.B.C. introduce teletext.*	*Sony first introduce the 'Walkman' personal stereo player.*	*Poll Tax reintroduced; leads to mass riots and is withdrawn.*	*Tories lose general election to Labour, ending a record 18 years in power.*
1973	**1979**	**1982**	**1991**	
Britain joins the E.E.C. (the Common Market).	*Margaret Thatcher becomes first woman Prime Minister.*	*The Falklands War.*	*The Gulf War.*	

🏛 GOVERNMENT　　🥄 HEALTH & MEDICINE　　⚖ JUSTICE　　✝ RELIGION　　📏 SCIENCE

HOUSE OF HANOVER & WINDSOR

THE HANOVERIANS

☙ George I
1714–1725
m Sophia of Celle
d.1726

☙ George II
1727–1760
m Caroline of Anspach
d.1737

Frederick Lewis, Prince of Wales
d.1751
m Augusta of Saxe-Gotha
d.1772

☙ George III
1760–1820
m Sophia Charlotte of Mecklenburg-Strelitz
d.1818

☙ George IV
1820–1830
m Caroline of Brunswick
│
Charlotte
d.1817

☙ William IV
1830–1837
m Adelaide of Saxe-Meiningen
1792–1849
│
Charlotte
d.1819
│
Elizabeth
d.1821

Edward Duke of Kent
d.1820

m Victoria of Saxe-Coburg-Saalfeld
d.1861

☙ Victoria
1837–1901
m Albert of Saxe-Coburg-Gotha
Prince Consort
d.1861

☙ Edward VII
1901–1910

☙ George V
1910–1936

☙ Edward VIII
Duke of Windsor
1936 (d.1972)

☙ George VI
1936–1952

☙ Elizabeth II

THE WINDSORS

To ensure that the throne remained in Protestant hands, the Act of Settlement was passed in 1701. It was decided that the crown would pass to the Protestant Electress of Hanover, Sophia (who was James I's granddaughter) or her descendants. When Sophia died in 1714, her son George became heir to the English throne. In 1917, George V changed the family name to Windsor because of the anti-German feeling at the time, and so began a new dynastic line.

ACKNOWLEDGEMENTS

This Series is dedicated to J. Allan Twiggs whose enthusiasm for British History has inspired these four books.
We would also like to thank: Graham Rich, Tracey Pennington, and Peter Done for their assistance.

ticktock Publishing Ltd., The Offices in the Square, Hadlow, Kent TN11 ODD, UK

A CIP Catalogue for this book is available from the British Library. ISBN 1 86007 021 3

Acknowledgements: Picture Credits t=top, b=bottom, c=centre, l=left, r=right, OFC=outside front cover, IFC=inside front cover, IBC=inside back cover, OBC=outside back cover.

AKG, London: 19tr, 22tl, 28t, 28br & OBC. Ancient Art & Architecture Library: 3br, 4tl, 8t & OBC, 9b. Barnaby Picture Library: 20b, 27t, 30tl & OBC. Bridgeman Art Library: 5t & IFC, 4r, 9t, 15t & OFC, 19l & br, 30tr ('True Blue c Ruskin Spear 191101990). E.T. Archive: 13t. Mary Evans Picture Library: 2tl, 2br, 6br, 8b, 10bl & br, 12tl, 13br, 14 cr, 14bl & detail, 15br, 16t, 18tl & bc, 20tl, 21t & br, 24tl, cl, cr, &32 bl, 25tr & br, 26tl &cc, 27cl & br, 30c, 31tr. Chris Fairclough/Image Select: 5br, 11bc. Fine Art Photographic Library: 14t. Image Select: 22c, 23t & OBC, bl, br &OBC. Imperial War Museum: 29 br. London Features International: 31 bl. Military Photo Library: 28bc Crown Copyright - ABF Museum, 29tc & OFC (c) Geoff Lee, 30bl & OBC (c) Robin Adshead. National Maritime Museum: 3t, 6cl, 7t, 12br, 20c & OFC. National Portrait Gallery (London): 11r & OFC. National Railway Museum: 10t & OBC. Press Association: 16b. Ann Ronan / Image Select: 7b, 17t.

Every effort has been made to trace the copyright holders and we apologise in advance for any unintentional omissions.
We would be pleased to insert the appropriate acknowledgement in any subsequent edition of this publication.
Printed in Italy

A 1,000 YEARS OF BRITISH HISTORY - THE MILLENNIUM SERIES

BOOK I (1,000~1399)

BOOK II (1399~1603)

BOOK III (1603~1714)

BOOK IV (1714~ present day)